This book is base[...] advice column in [...] since the newspa[...] 1988, 'Dear Jo' has been one of its most popular features. People writing vary in age from five to sixteen, but *Dear Jo Plus* deals with those letters from teenagers who are seeking advice on the many issues and problems relating to the years eleven to sixteen.

To protect readers' anonymity, all the names have been changed. The letters have been divided by subject into sections and the number of letters in each section reflects the number of letters the paper receives about the subject. Topics which occur less frequently have been included in the 'Pic 'n Mix' section towards the end of the book. A list of Useful Addresses is included for young people who seek further help.

'Jo' is the pseudonym of a practising child psychotherapist with three young children of her own. She has written the column since its early days.

Early Times is an independent newspaper for young people which was launched in January 1988. With an estimated readership of 200,000 the paper has attracted much press coverage, particularly for its Press Gang interviews of Margaret Thatcher, Neil Kinnock and other well-known politicians and personalities.

EARLY 🌳 TIMES
The independent newspaper for young people

DEAR JO PLUS

*Letters to and from an
advice columnist*

PENGUIN BOOKS

PENGUIN BOOKS

Published by the Penguin Group
27 Wrights Lane, London W8 5TZ, England
Viking Penguin, a division of Penguin Books USA Inc.
375 Hudson Street, New York, New York 10014, USA
Penguin Books Australia Ltd, Ringwood, Victoria, Australia
Penguin Books Canada Ltd, 2801 John Street, Markham, Ontario,
Canada L3R 1B4
Penguin Books (NZ) Ltd, 182–190 Wairau Road, Auckland 10, New
Zealand

Penguin Books Ltd, Registered Offices: Harmondsworth, Middlesex,
England

This selection published in Penguin Books 1991
1 3 5 7 9 10 8 6 4 2

Early Times would like to acknowledge the invaluable work
of Gillian Denton in the preparation of this book.

Filmset in 10pt Monophoto Sabon

Made and printed in Great Britain by
Clays Ltd, St Ives plc

CONTENTS

I

FIRST TIMES

Growing up can be both painful and embarrassing. Many young people who write to me are worried by their first serious sexual feelings. Girls are worried about vaginal discharge when they feel sexy and boys about unwanted erections which they feel are visible to everyone on the bus or in the cinema queue. Both girls and boys worry about when it is 'right' to make love for the first time (that's a very hard one to answer), and they feel slightly out of control of the situation. Of course, this is not the case, although it's all too easy to get carried away when you are aroused. Worries about pregnancy also feature, even in letters from quite young readers.

Dear Jo,
I am 14, and in school all my class talk about masturbation. I think some of them do it. I don't know what it is and I feel left out. Please don't tell me to buy a book or anything, but I would like to know exactly what it means.

Max Bradshaw,
Petersfield, Hampshire

There are many slang words for masturbation, Max, such as wanking, playing with yourself, jerking off and so on. Probably you have heard some of these. Quite simply, masturbating means feeling your genitals in order to become sexually excited and sometimes (although not always) give yourself an orgasm. Once upon a time, people thought that masturbation was bad for you and some people even believed that it made you go blind. These old wives' tales are just that – old wives' tales. Masturbation does you no harm at all and no one should feel guilty or scared about it. Actually, it gives you a good feeling, and is an excellent way of getting to know your own body and the way it responds to sexual stimulus. *But*, and it's a big but, many boys and girls never feel the need to masturbate and there's nothing wrong with that either. It doesn't mean that you're never going to enjoy sex or that you are undersexed. We're all different.

Finally, Max, I *am* going to recommend a book for you to read. It's called *Make it Happy Make it Safe* by Jane Cousins-Mills and it's published by Penguin.

Dear Jo,

I am 15 and very worried indeed. I'm always getting a 'hard on' and this can be very embarrassing at times. I get one many times a day. I also masturbate which makes me feel really dirty. I have two older brothers and a younger brother and I don't think any of them have my problems. Please can you give me some advice on what to do.

Michael Weedon,
Weybridge, Surrey

I get many letters from boys of your age, Michael, with the same problem. You are definitely not alone, and I bet your older brothers have been through it all too. Ask them, if you're on good terms with them. I expect they'll sympathize.

As you probably know, you usually, but not always, get an erection (or hard on) when something has made you feel sexy. However, many boys in their early teens find that they get erections for no apparent reason at all, sometimes many times a day, and sometimes in the weirdest places – having tea with your gran, for example! There's no doubt that they can be embarrassing and it's not always possible to hide the fact that you're having one. Take heart. Sudden, often unwanted erections stop happening after a while. In the meantime, try thinking of something revolting, like your younger brother eating his baked beans, when you feel an erection coming. That'll soon help it to subside.

As for the masturbation, as I said in my previous answer, that is certainly not a problem and you have absolutely no need to feel guilty about it. Masturbating is not only normal, but also good for you. Doctors consider it to be a healthy release of pent-up feelings, especially in adolescence, and it's also a good way to be in touch with your own body. As long as it's done in private there's nothing to be ashamed of.

Dear Jo,
I keep having erections in front of the most ugly girl in the school. I think she knows it because she goes red and has asked me into the woods.

The only other person who knows is my friend Jonathon. He told me to ask her out, but I can't face it. Yesterday, this girl jumped on me while we were in the science lab and made me agree to meet her next Wednesday. I don't want to go, but I feel I have to. I know that she has told the girls in my class that I love her, but I do not. I don't know what to do. She follows me everywhere.

James Brody,
Devizes, Wiltshire

As I said in my previous reply, there's nothing wrong with getting erections, but they can be embarrassing. Probably, you got one once in front of this girl and now you're so self-conscious about it that you keep getting them. She may not know that you get erections, but she *has* sussed out that you feel uncomfortable near her and has put this down, quite understandably in the circumstances, to you fancying her. If you really don't, then whatever Jonathon says and she wants, it would be hurtful and silly to lead her on. This is definitely a case of being cruel to be kind. If you can't bear to tell her face to face that you don't want to meet her, then write her a little note and put it in her locker before school one day. Tell her that you're happy to be friends with her as you are with lots of other girls, but that you can't cope with a heavier sort of relationship.

Perhaps she's making such a big thing of all this because she's not very happy with her appearance and is very unsure of herself.

Dear Jo,
I am 15. I have got a new boyfriend called James whom I love dearly. I would like to make love with him but I don't know how far he wants to go. What should I do? Please give me some good advice because many of my friends have the same problem.

Carly Nicholson,
Bridgwater, Somerset

How lovely to have a new boyfriend you're so fond of. When we feel like that about someone it's very natural to want to make love with them. Probably, when you're kissing and cuddling you want to go on and on, but there are a couple of points to consider very carefully.

The first is that it is against the law for people under 16 to have sex. Sixteen is the Age of Consent in Britain, so sex before that age is breaking the law.

Another equally important point to remember, is that sex leads to pregnancy. Before you embark upon your first sexual encounter you should be quite certain that you have both investigated and chosen the safest form of contraception.

Deciding whether or not to have sex with someone is a pretty tough decision and you'll really have to go into your own feelings and values before you make it. Whatever happens, don't be pressured into it by anyone.

If you're asking me (and I think you are) whether I think you're old enough to have sex, then I'm afraid that the answer (quite apart from the legal question) must be no. Although the age when you are able to cope with a sexual relationship varies from person to person, on balance, my personal view is that there are few girls (or boys) of 15 who are mature enough to cope with all the problems and demands which a sexual relationship can give you. It takes years to sort out sexual feelings and values and you certainly haven't come to grips with them all at 15.

The fact that you don't know what James wants does really underline my feeling that neither of you are really ready for sex yet. Talk it over with him. He should certainly be part of the decision-making process and you should be very sure of his feelings for you.

Dear Jo,
I'm 12 years old and have a serious problem. I have a great sexual desire to make love to a girl and have wanted to for about a year. I have tried to do it but I have not got very far with it. I would desperately like to.

I'm not fully developed but I'm not far from it. I need help.

Jason Johnson,
Shrewsbury, Shropshire

Your problem, Jason, is that you are growing up fast. Your hormones are in overdrive but you're not yet, as you say yourself, quite fully developed so you can't quite get it together at the moment.

Girls you meet will seem attractive to you now and you'll find many of them a turn on. I wasn't quite sure from your letter whether you fancy and have tried to make love with one girl in particular or just someone who happened to be around. Either way, when your body's ready to make love you will be able to. But you've got loads of time yet; don't rush it. And remember that you'll get a lot more out of it if you wait for the right person.

Dear Jo,
I am in my early teens and recently my boyfriend and I got very involved with each other. We made love and he did not wear a condom. Now I am afraid that I am pregnant. I don't know how to tell Mum. Can you help me?

Michelle Robson,
Bath, Avon

If you have been menstruating (having periods) for some time, then I'm afraid that it is possible that you are pregnant. Of course, it would be best to tell your mum as soon as possible; I'm sure she'll be able to advise you. But if you really feel you can't confide in her, or you don't want to in case it's just a false alarm, then contact the Brook Advisory Centre. I think that the nearest branch to you is in Bristol. The address and telephone number of the central office is at the back of this book. Phone, write or call in. They are very sympathetic to young people and anything you tell them will be in the strictest confidence.

Don't delay though Michelle; the sooner you know for sure whether or not you are pregnant, the sooner you can decide what course of action to take. Do consult your parents though. You could be surprised at how understanding they'll be.

Dear Jo,
I am a 14-year-old boy and recently I had sex with a 15-year-old girl in the showers at school, late, after swimming. She was wearing a white almost see-through costume and I couldn't resist it. Now I think that she may be pregnant, but I can't ask her because I'm so embarrassed.

Damian Rodgers,
Basingstoke, Hampshire

What a pity that your swimming classes were not better supervised. I can understand that you both must have been very tempted. However, your friend may not be pregnant. I have a feeling she would have told you if she were. How long is it since the incident took place? Have you thought of just approaching her and saying something like, 'I'm sorry for what happened the other week. Are you OK?' If she is pregnant, this will give her an opportunity to tell you, and you can decide together which adult you are going to tell and what you are going to do about it. Let's hope she's not, but whether she is pregnant or not, you do know, don't you, that it is illegal to have sexual intercourse with a girl under 16?

Dear Jo,
Please help as I have done an awful thing. A few months ago, just out of curiosity, I rang up a Stripline. When I got through, I was so embarrassed that I didn't wait to hear anything, but put the phone down. That night I started masturbating. I have also noticed that I have some vaginal discharge sometimes which makes my pants wet. I have also developed a mad crush on a boy in my class. He only has to speak and I go red. By the way, I am 12. Have all these things started from just one phone call?

Ginny Reeves,
Orpington, Kent

What a good job you were sensible and mature enough to put the phone down when you did, Ginny. Most people think that these phone lines should be abolished and many of them operate illegally you know. It might be a good idea to tell your mum, or your teacher or any adult that you like and respect about this one. You could even call your local Citizens' Advice Bureau or drop them a line. You don't have to tell them that you rang the number up. Many of these chatlines are being investigated by the police at the moment.

The phone call certainly didn't start off all the other things you mention. Masturbating, occasionally having a small vaginal secretion and having a crush on the boy in your class are all very normal indications that you are growing up fast. There is nothing wrong with masturbating so don't worry about it. I have discussed it with a couple of other people in this book.

Try wearing one of those very small panty liners in your pants and that will stop them getting wet when you discharge a small amount of fluid. There's no need to worry about it. Unless it smells unpleasant, and/or is a funny colour, it's just normal vaginal lubrication.

Having a crush on someone is a very good way to start learning about love. You'll find soon (maybe with this boy) that you want your feelings to be returned – if they are, then it stops being a crush and starts being a relationship. I hope things work out for you.

Dear Jo,
A couple of times last week I woke up to find that I had wet myself. I was so ashamed that I didn't tell my mum but washed and dried my pyjamas without her knowing. I'm worried that this is going to happen again. I'm 13 and I haven't wet myself since I was nine. I told my friend Jamie and he was relieved because he said the same thing had happened to him. Can you help?

Piers Fielding,
Rochester, Kent

It sounds to me, Piers, as if both you and Jamie are having wet dreams, and this doesn't mean that you have urinated in your sleep. There are some dreams, and they are usually, but not always, sexy ones, which make a boy ejaculate semen in his sleep; that's the substance that is all over your pyjamas. The good side to having wet dreams, is that it's a sure sign that you are reaching sexual maturity. Not all boys have them. Some only have them when they start to masturbate or have sex. Either way is quite normal and you don't need to feel ashamed.

If you really don't like waking up in this way, try keeping your underpants on at bedtime. You can easily rinse them through in the morning.

Dear Jo,
We are two girls and we go to boarding school. We have a funny problem. In gym, at school, when we climb up the ropes we get a really nice feeling. We just want to go on climbing and hanging there. Why do we feel like this?

Amanda Simmonds,
Petra Frankel,
Hampton, Middlesex

Well, I'm pretty sure that this feeling doesn't happen because you've managed to climb up the ropes! Sense of achievement doesn't make you feel quite like this! My guess is that as you climb, the rope is rubbing your clitoris – a small knob in the vulva (outer sex organs) – which is extremely sensitive. Playing around with your clitoris is one way for a female to masturbate. It can give you a really nice feeling and make you feel very sexy and I suspect that the rope rubbing you is doing just that.

Dear Jo,
My parents live in Hong Kong and I go to boarding school in England. I like it very much, but the trouble is that there are certain things that I don't know about growing up,

and I don't like to ask my mum on the telephone in case someone is listening. I understand the basic facts of life but I don't know what 'having an affair' is or what 'having it off' is. Please tell me what they mean, because I am sure that lots of other girls want to know as well.

Katie Colquhoun,
Brighton, Sussex

I know exactly what you mean about talking to your mum on the telephone, especially over such a long distance. It would probably be a pretty expensive call!

In a nutshell, 'having an affair' means a situation in which a man and a woman enjoy a sexual relationship even though one or both partners are married to other people.

'Having it off' means having sexual intercourse. We all use slang for all sorts of things. It's like shorthand; it helps us express ourselves quickly. But I do think that 'having it off' is a pretty unimaginative choice of words for what is often an extremely enjoyable, and sometimes even beautiful, experience. I prefer 'making love'. You can decide when you're older which term you prefer.

Dear Jo,
A couple of days ago I was playing in my mum's bedroom, when I came across this box under her bed which had what looked like a small rubber bowl in it. When I asked her what it was, she told me that it was her cap, which stopped her having any more babies. Now I'm a bit confused, because I thought that what stopped you having

babies were condoms like you see advertised in the papers and on the television. What's the difference? I don't like to ask my mum because I think she thinks I already know and I feel a bit of a fool. Please help.

Claire Roper,
Salisbury, Wiltshire

As I'm sure you know, Claire, there is more than one type of contraceptive, or birth control device. What your mum uses is a diaphragm or Dutch cap. This fits inside the vagina and closes off the entrance to the womb so that no sperm can enter the womb. Every woman has to be specially fitted for one so you can't just go and buy one in a chemist. They are pretty safe, especially when used with a special jelly or cream which kills sperm.

A condom has the same function as a cap – birth control – but it works the other way round. It looks like a thin rubber balloon and fits on to an erect penis. It stops sperm entering the vagina. It has one other huge advantage. It stops the spread of sexually transmitted diseases like AIDS.

If you do want to understand more about contraception, Claire, do ask your mum. I'm sure she'll be only too glad to tell you, and you sound to me as if you've got a pretty good relationship with her.

Dear Jo,
I've been invited to a party next week where the boys are going to be a bit older than I am (I'm 13). My best friend says there's going to be lots of French kissing. I'm really

worried about this because I'm not too sure exactly what it is. Can you help?

Gail Pigeon,
Northwich, Cheshire

First of all, Gail, there's only going to be French kissing if you and any boy you meet at the party want there to be. You really are under no obligation to French kiss to order or even to kiss at all if you don't want to!

French kissing, is kissing with your mouths slightly apart and using your tongues to explore each other's mouths. It is a *very* personal form of contact and one which you probably wouldn't want to try with someone you have only just met. In addition, French kissing carries a very small risk of getting AIDS so you should be very sure of your partner before you try it.

Don't feel you have to do anything that you don't want to just because you're afraid of being thought wimpish or because you think everyone else is doing it. I bet they're not! Enjoy the party.

Dear Jo,
What is foreplay and am I too young to do it? I'm eight.

Peter Philips,
London

Foreplay is one way of enjoying sex. It means all the cuddling and kissing that couples do when they are making love. It usually ends in sexual intercourse but it doesn't have to.

I do actually think you're too young to enjoy foreplay yet, Peter. Wait a few more years until you really *want* to do it. Meanwhile, enjoy lots of kisses and cuddles with your dad and mum. Physical affection makes you feel good however old you are.

2

MENSTRUATION

I am always amazed at how many letters I receive on this subject, and because I receive so many I am going to devote a whole section to it. (Sorry, lads!)

Many years ago, of course, menstruation was a very taboo topic; everyone knew that women had periods but they were something that women put up with and probably didn't even mention to each other. Menstruation even had a negative slang name – the curse. Today, things have improved slightly; menstruation is now out in the open and advertisements for menstrual products such as tampons and pads are not uncommon in the newspapers and on television.

However, it seems from your letters that periods are still regarded negatively. This may be because your mums have never really talked to you about it, perhaps because they're not too sure how to explain what it is. A recent report in the US showed that 75% of women couldn't explain clearly to a 12-year-old what happens when we menstruate. I imagine that the situation is much the same in Britain. I hope my explanation will make things a little clearer and help you to feel more positive about becoming *a woman, and that the selection of letters and answers published will cover any queries you may have.*

Menstruation is the technical word for a period. It comes from the Latin word menses, *which means month. Very few people get their period exactly every 28 days. It's usually a little bit more or a little bit less.*

The inside walls of the uterus (womb) are covered with a special lining. Every month, or thereabouts, when a girl reaches puberty, an ovum (egg) ripens in the ovary, and the lining gets itself ready in case the egg becomes fertilized (by a sperm during sex), in which case it will plant itself in the lining. The lining becomes thicker, it develops new blood passages and spongy tissue grows. If the egg is not fertilized, then this new lining is not needed and the womb gradually begins to get rid of it. This shedding of the lining is menstruation. The blood doesn't come out all at once but trickles out over a number of days. The length of time (a period) varies from person to person.

Once the bleeding has stopped, the uterus starts growing a new lining in case it is needed for next month's ripe egg, and the whole process begins again.

OK? Now let's get down to your letters.

Dear Jo,

We are two school girls who have some questions to ask you. We are at a boarding school and we are both worried about what will happen if our periods start while we are at school. Our mothers have explained to us what happens but we are still worried.

Also, neither of us masturbate, but if we did, would it help us to get our periods earlier, or would it make no difference? Is masturbating disgusting?

When we get our periods, at what age do you think we should use tampons? Our mothers have given us towels, but they are really long and we think that if we wear them they will stick out and show. Is there any way we can cut them?

I know that I am not the same as my mum, but she says I will still get a large flow like her, so if we did cut our towels would I have to change mine more often?

This is very serious. Please help.

Caroline Tozer,
Henrietta McGuire,
Chesham, Buckinghamshire

Well, there are certainly a lot of questions from you two. What a good job you've got each other to discuss things with. I'll go through your points one by one.

I can see that there are different problems when you reach puberty at boarding school. It must be quite difficult not having your mum available for a chat. I expect each boarding school operates quite differently, but I'm sure that the school matron or the house-mother is quite prepared for girls reaching puberty and no doubt keeps a stock of spare towels or tampons in case any girl runs out or is unprepared for menstruation.

I have answered questions about masturbation in the first section of this book. There is absolutely nothing disgusting about it and it is certainly nothing to be ashamed of. Neither will it encourage your periods to come early. They'll arrive when your body is good and ready. However, because you have reached puberty (periods sometimes don't appear until two years after puberty has begun) you may feel inclined to masturbate. If so, do so; there's nothing wrong with it.

In general, most doctors advise girls to wear towels for the first few months, until the cycle has become established. After that, there is no reason why you shouldn't start wearing tampons. Many manufacturers make especially thin ones for young girls. If you follow the instructions carefully you'll soon get the hang of inserting them. It takes practice, and you may waste a few to begin with, but you'll soon find a position for inserting them that is comfortable for you.

Some girls wear towels, and sometimes tampons as well, at the beginning of their period and then tampons when the blood flow has slackened off a bit. Don't cut the towels; they are filled with soft material like cotton wool and would soon fall apart. Many short towels are now available and certainly won't show, even when you are doing games or gym. When you get a chance, visit your biggest local chemist and have a snoop around the shelves. You'll soon find out exactly what's available and what suits you best.

Your flow won't be lighter than your mum's because you are younger, but it might be lighter because you are a different person. Because your mum has a heavy flow does not mean that you will. You might, but then again you might not. You'll probably also find, to begin with, that the amount of blood you lose varies slightly, from month to month, until your cycle settles down. You'll soon get used to knowing when it is time to change your tampon or towel. It is best to do it sooner rather than later, so that you are always confident that the blood flow is contained. You will also have to wash more often at this time of the month. Although the menstrual blood itself is not in the least smelly, by the time it reaches your towel it will have encountered many germs in the vagina and in the air, and because germs develop fast in the rich blood it will develop an odour.

Dear Jo,
Please help, I am really scared. One day after school, I took my knickers off and found left on them a bloody mess. Is this my period or what? Should I go to the doctor as he knows our family? I'm too embarrassed to ask my mum. I have never had this before, and I am only 11. My sister is older than me and she has not started yet. What should I do?

Samantha Duval,
Manchester

This could indeed be your first period. Sometimes, first periods are comparatively light and there is not excessive blood loss. You are certainly not too young to be having a period. Some girls start as early as nine and some as late as 16. Most begin somewhere in the middle. The fact that your sister has not begun yet is largely irrelevant – you are two different people, and although sisters do sometimes begin at roughly the same age, that is by no means always the case.

Do stop being embarrassed and tell your mother. She will then be able to help you sort out what you need in preparation for the next period. If this doesn't appear, don't be alarmed; periods are often not very regular to begin with. You certainly don't need to bother your doctor, unless you are experiencing other signs of illness. If you are, you must tell your mum and let her decide what is to be done.

Dear Jo,
Please help, I have got a really big problem. I am 11 and I go to boarding school. Everyone keeps on teasing me, because I am very mature and I have my periods.

One time, they came in while I was in the bath and pulled me out. Everyone stared at me and I was so embarrassed that I started to cry. I am so scared I can't talk to my friends or my parents. What can I do?

Lara Carnforth,
Haslemere, Surrey

It's a sad fact of human nature, Lara, that people tend to pick on the odd one out. Unfortunately, at the moment, that's you. Of course, it won't be for long. Soon all your friends will be catching up with you and the odd girls out will be those who haven't started their periods. Do be nice to them!

I must say I think these girls who bullied you sound extremely unpleasant. Presumably, your friends were not around to support you. Bullies are always cowards you know, and it doesn't usually take much to stop them in their tracks.

If they persist in victimizing you, I feel that you must tell a teacher. You're not telling tales, you're reporting an unpleasant incident which should not have taken place. Try to see a teacher at a time when you are not conspicuous; you don't want these cruel girls to accuse you of sneaking.

Do confide in your friends and your parents; they'll sympathize and may be able to help.

Dear Jo,
I am quite upset because I have started my periods at the age of ten and none of my friends have. Whenever I have one, my mum tells me to use a stick up tampon, and last time it got stuck so that the doctor had to pull it out, so you can see why I am upset.

Harriet Rodgers,
Chard, Somerset

What an unpleasant experience for you. I have heard before of tampons that get 'lost' in the vagina. What actually happens is that the string that is attached to the end of the tampon goes too far up into the vagina so that you can't see or feel the string. I expect you panicked a bit Harriet. If you can relax it's actually quite a simple matter to get the tampon out. You just have to reach up with your fingers and pull it out. It may be easier if you squat. So if it should ever happen again you'll know what to do.

However, for the time being, Harriet, I think it would be a good idea if you used towels until you become quite at ease with your periods. Have a word with your mum, and tell her what you've told me. I'm sure she'll understand.

Dear Jo,
My friend and I are fed up with this boy in our class who thinks that periods are a joke and keeps teasing us for having them. What can we do?

Rebecca Paige,
Sally Mount,
Ipswich, Suffolk

This boy probably doesn't know what a period is, so he's covering himself by making fun of you. Try to ignore him if possible; if not, try and have a word with one of his friends whom you like, and see if he can get this boy to stop. Failing that, you can either put up with it (he will stop eventually if he sees he's not getting to you) or you can tell him that you've had enough and that you're going to complain to a teacher – then do it!

Dear Jo,
I have a bad problem. I have started my periods but I don't know how to tell my mum. I've coped by myself so far,

using her tampons, but I'm worried they may not be right for me.

I'm the youngest in my family, and I think my mum still thinks of me as a baby even though I'm 12. We have talked about periods but it was a long time ago and I think my mum'll have forgotten. How can I tell her?

Sarah Innes,
Perivale, Middlesex

I think your mum would be pretty hurt if she thought you couldn't confide in her. If you are the baby of the family she probably will find it quite hard to admit that you are growing up fast, but she'll cope with that and I'm sure will be anxious to help you sort everything out. Her tampons may be too big for you. You should probably get the narrowest sort.

The fact that she has explained periods to you means that she has probably been prepared for a long time for you to make your announcement. Maybe she hasn't mentioned them to you recently, because she didn't want to appear to be pressuring you, or maybe she was simply too busy. Whatever the reason you must talk to her now Sarah; I'm sure once you start it'll be fine. It's often a bit embarrassing talking to parents about very intimate things, however close you may be.

Dear Jo,
Recently, I heard my sister Kate talking in the bathroom to her best friend Rosie and she told her that she'd been very worried because she was giving off a nasty liquid and

it smelt but that it was OK now because it was just a tampon; I didn't catch any more. I can't ask her what she meant because I don't want her to know that I've been listening. What do you think she meant? Do you think she's really all right?

Charlotte Ashley,
Solihull, West Midlands

Well, of course I don't *know* what Kate and Rosie were talking about because I wasn't listening, but I could hazard a guess. Some young women sometimes find wearing tampons so comfortable that they forget that they're there, particularly towards the end of a period. They leave the last one in, and if it is not removed for some time, it will eventually cause a foul odour and probably a discharge as well. As soon as the forgotten tampon is removed, both odour and discharge clear up pretty well instantly.

If you're still worried about your sister, Charlotte, you'll just have to own up and ask her!

Dear Jo,
I am 14 and I get quite bad period pains before I have a period. Once it comes I feel all right. My friend's mother says I shouldn't take any exercise before or during a period because it will make it worse. The trouble is, that in the summer I play a lot of tennis. I used to worry that I might bleed and it would show, but this has never happened. Should I give up tennis while I am having my period?

Julie Barnes,
Cambridge

With the state of British tennis today, I think you should play as much as possible, Julie! But seriously; you can do exactly the same things before and during a period as you can at any other time. There are many old wives' tales about exercise causing a heavier flow, or increased period pains or a longer period but none of these are true. In fact, exercise sometimes helps to relieve period pains.

Dear Jo,
I am 15, and I started my periods when I was 12. I'm a bit worried now though, because I love children and I want to have four, but my friend told me that people whose periods aren't very regular, can't have children. My periods only come about every seven weeks and sometimes they miss out altogether. Is my friend right?

Claudine Brown,
Southampton, Hampshire

Not all women have periods every 28 days, but most are fairly regular to within a few days either side. There are a number of things that can make your period late or cease altogether, for example, worry, crash dieting, illness and so on. Irregular periods do not mean that you can't have children, but there may be something wrong that could easily be put right. It would be best to see your doctor and have a long chat. Don't just go along at normal surgery time; make an appointment and then he or she will be able to devote some time to you. Take your mum or a friend along for a bit of support and in case you don't understand everything that is said (doctors sometimes get a bit technical), and between two of you, you should be able to remember everything.

Dear Jo,
I have my periods and they are quite regular, but in between each one I sometimes get a few spots of blood on my pants. Am I all right?

Anne-Marie Raleigh,
Port Talbot, West Glamorgan

'Spotting' is not at all unusual. It usually occurs around the time of ovulation. You can work out if this is the case by keeping a simple chart of your periods. Count back two weeks from the start of a period and if this is when the spotting happened, it is probably connected with ovulation and isn't anything to worry about.

3

LOOKS

As boys and girls reach adolescence, their bodies and their faces begin to change. Sometimes this can give a great deal of pleasure but more often than not, it is a cause of embarrassment, dissatisfaction and even despair.

Many of the letters I receive from girls are about the development of their breasts. Concern about size seems to be divided in about equal measure between those of you who think your bust measurement rivals Samantha Fox and those of you for whom even a 30AA cup seems to be too big.

Boys are clearly concerned about personal hygiene, skin and weight, and you're all concerned about a number of other things as well, as these letters show.

Dear Jo,

I'm 13 and not too bad looking except for one terrible thing. I have these hideous zits. I've tried to hide them but it doesn't really work. Most of them are on my face but I've got a few on my back too. No girl is ever going to look at me while I've got these. Help!

Gary Newburn,
Colchester, Essex

There is no getting away from the fact that spots are pretty unsightly. Unfortunately, teenage acne is caused by an excess of sebum blocking the pores of the skin. Production of sebum during adolescence tends to be vigorous and is a reaction to the many hormonal changes that are going on at this time.

People used to think that washing often helped to cure acne, but we now know that it sometimes has the opposite effect. Rather than drying up the spots, washing often stimulates the sebaceous glands, and oil production is actually encouraged.

A very healthy, non-fat diet may help, Gary, and it'll make you feel good anyway. Don't waste your money on chemical products to cure the spots because by and large they don't work.

I'm afraid there's not much comfort I can give you, except that you will grow out of it, that many others are in the same boat (90% of teenagers suffer from spots to some extent), and your spots are much more noticeable to you than to anyone else.

Covering them up won't do them any harm. There are

some good cover-ups on the market and many of them are not too expensive.

Good luck and remember — they will go eventually!

Dear Jo,
I have a huge problem — and I mean huge! I am growing very big boobs. I don't really mind, but the trouble is I don't want to wear a bra. I find that they are very uncomfortable and I don't like how they look. My mum says that if I don't, my boobs will become all droopy. Is she right? They don't droop at the moment.

Charly Jackson,
Midhurst, Sussex

Many women with big breasts prefer to wear a bra because they find it more comfortable. Maybe the bras you have tried have not been the correct size. Perhaps you should go and get one specially fitted. Most big department stores have assistants who are trained in this. You can certainly buy very pretty bras indeed, but they do tend to be very expensive.

If you really hate wearing a bra, there is no reason why you should. You don't need the support at the moment, because your muscles are young and strong. But your mum is right in a sense; if you don't wear a bra, your breasts will tend to droop more as you get older and your muscles get weaker. But then who's to say that droopy breasts are worse than any other kind?

Perhaps the answer is to wear a bra sometimes — when

you are playing sports, for example, and leave it off at others. I feel it's really up to you, Charly.

Dear Jo,
I am nearly 12 years old and the youngest in my year and in the whole school because I've just started secondary school. I have this massive problem. I have the biggest boobs in the whole of the first and second years put together. I'm even bigger than some of the fifth years. I have a medium figure and am quite tall and good-looking, but big on top. One boy fancies me and his friends told me and even a teacher heard. I am quite embarrassed. One boy said I should feel proud.

Chelsea Willmott,
London

Well, Chelsea, I think that inside you do feel quite proud. You've obviously got a lovely figure and are beginning to realize that boys fancy you – and that's fine. Perhaps other girls have made you think that you should be embarrassed by your big breasts. You shouldn't, of course, any more than you should feel embarrassed if you have very small breasts. The trouble is, that because we see so many big-busted, beautiful women on television and in the newspapers, it's very easy to get the idea that big breasts are 'better' or more sexy than small ones, and that's nonsense of course.

I hope you don't feel that the boy fancies you just because you're well-developed. I expect he thinks you're very nice too. Try not to think too much about your breasts, Chelsea. They're not the most important part of you.

Dear Jo,
I have a very unusual problem. I am a ten-year-old girl and I have very big boobs. One of the girls in my class, who also has big boobs, doesn't mind, because they are small for a girl of her age although big for my class. She wears a bra every Monday and Friday when we have sports lessons, and she is a size 32AA. I wear bras more often and I am a 34AA. It gets on my nerves, because I go to a mixed school and the boys keep pinging my bra and the other girls ask me if it's stuffed. Please help.

Natalie Ward,
Portsmouth, Hampshire

If you've read the rest of this chapter, Natalie, you'll know by now that your predicament is not unusual. What really seems to be getting to you is the reactions of your classmates, both male and female.

The other girls are probably reacting in this way because they are not quite as well-developed as you yet and maybe they would like to be. It sounds like a bit of jealousy to me. As soon as they start developing too, this kind of teasing will stop. In the meantime, when they tease you, just show that you find it rather boring, and don't rise to their bait.

The boys are behaving like this, partly because they're not yet used to their classmates wearing bras and you are a bit of a novelty, and partly because you let them see that it gets on your nerves, which I can well understand. Perhaps the answer is not to wear a bra at school for a bit. Take one with you to put on for games, and otherwise only wear it in the evening and at weekends.

When your female classmates catch up with you and start wearing bras too, your problems will be over. The boys can't possibly go round pinging bras all day long. They'd soon find it very boring.

Dear Jo,
I am nearly ten, and I want boobs badly. At the moment there is no sign of them so my friend and I stuff our bras with tissues to make us look good and I think we do. The trouble is that I want a boyfriend, and boys only fancy girls with big boobs. What can I do?

Susanna Phillips,
East Molesey, Surrey

Obviously you can't make your breasts grow any faster, Susanna, so if it makes you feel better, I should go on stuffing tissues into your bra. However, please don't think that boys only fancy girls with big breasts; that really isn't true. As you get older, you'll see that some boys like girls with large breasts and some boys don't. The nicest boys will like you whether you have small or large breasts. Why don't you concentrate for the moment on getting to know some boys a bit better. Join a club where you'll soon get to know lots of boys and girls. Going around in a gang is a great way to start to get to know the opposite sex.

Dear Jo,
I am very worried because I have very large breasts. I am
11 years old and I am a size 36B bra. What really worries
me is that I have stretch marks on my left breast, and I
noticed the other day that some are coming on my right
one too. I thought you only got stretch marks after you
had had a child. Please tell me if there is any way I can
make them go away.

Georgia Andrews,
Northampton

Some young people do develop stretch marks, purplish or
white lines on their skin, during puberty. This happens
because the skin is stretched too much when you grow
very rapidly and it loses its elastic quality, just as happens
when your breasts grow during pregnancy. If you've put
on a lot of weight all over recently, Georgia, this can also
cause stretch marks. In many cases these marks fade as
you get older and stop growing at quite such a rate. Try
not to worry too much about them. At your age, they are
very likely to fade quickly.

Dear Jo,
I am 14 and not too bad-looking, but I get dandruff. When
I come back from washing my hair, I go to bed and in the
morning, my pillow is covered with white flaky stuff. It
doesn't show too much in my hair because I am fair, but it
does get on my clothes which I find very embarrassing. I've

tried most of the shampoos and they don't seem to work. Is there anything else I can try?

Ben Dunsmore,
Lewes, Sussex

Dandruff is dead flakes of skin caused by a disorder of the glands in the scalp that secrete oil. There may be too little oil which causes dry, brittle hair and white flakes of skin, or more often too much, making hair greasy and causing yellow flakes of dandruff. Washing hair frequently is the answer; with a detergent shampoo if your hair is greasy, and a mild, baby shampoo if it is dry. Whichever it is, it is essential to remember to *rinse* your hair properly.

If following this regime for a bit doesn't work, Ben, then I suggest visiting your doctor. He or she may be able to prescribe some pills which you can take for a short time and which regulate the production of oil.

Dear Jo,
I have a rather large birthmark on my body, but it is not funny. I don't like wearing shorts and I avoid showers at school. Only my family know about it, but soon my friends are bound to discover it and I am worried. They will probably lose interest in me and I know I will get teased.

What can I do?

Nils Persson,
Cleveland

Do try to come to terms with that birthmark as quickly as possible, Nils. If you treat it as an unacceptable part of your body, your friends will react in the same way.

I do understand that you want to keep your mark covered up most of the time, but when this is not possible, try to be really casual about it and explain that it's just something you were born with. If you help your friends to understand they will soon be unconcerned about it and so will you. If any friend keeps teasing you, then he's not much of a friend, is he?

Dear Jo,
I am 15 years old and I am about to start attending college. I have a major problem. Can you help me please?

I have a tattoo on my right hand which indicates that I come from Rosyth.

I believe that this will cause me trouble, as most of the students live in rival areas. What can you suggest?

Duncan Cameron,
Rosyth, Fife

Being the world's most squeamish individual, I certainly don't envy you. The thought of having a tattoo done in the first place would send me running out of town. Having one removed is worse still.

I spoke to someone in the plastic surgery department of a London hospital. She explained that the standard treatment for removing tattoos, is to cut out the piece of skin with the tattoo, and graft on a fresh piece of skin from another part of your body, usually the inner thigh.

This means two small operations which can be done under a local anaesthetic (only those areas of your body are numbed, so you don't have to be put to sleep). You can be in and out of hospital on the same day.

However, skin grafts can leave scars and the new skin is not likely to exactly match the skin on the rest of your hand. If you look closely, you'll see that the skin looks different on each part of your body.

If that hasn't put you off, then go to see your family doctor. Explain about the tattoo and ask to be referred to the plastic surgery clinic of the nearest hospital. Not all hospitals have these clinics, so you may have to travel a bit. They would discuss things with you on a first visit and may make other suggestions.

If you don't really want the tattoo removed, then you'll have to tell your college mates that you had it done when you were younger, that you regret it and that it doesn't mean anything.

4

KICKING THE HABIT

There are some habits left over from childhood which when taken into adolescence become embarrassing and socially unacceptable. Most of these are perfectly harmless, like thumb-sucking, but are not always easy to give up.

There are other habits many young people pick up as they get older which are equally hard to give up. We all know how difficult it is to be the odd one out, to say 'no' when everyone else has said 'yes'; but many of these habits are both addictive and in some cases potentially very dangerous indeed.

Dear Jo,
Please help. I am 14 years old and I have a very annoying and distressing problem. Whenever I laugh, I wet myself uncontrollably. This makes me feel very uncomfortable and there is little that I can do about it. Is this just a bad habit I have got into? I don't want to see a doctor as I would be too embarrassed.

Serena Parsons,
St Albans, Hertfordshire

I'm afraid that I do have to suggest that you go to the doctor, Serena.

I spoke to a urologist (kidney and bladder specialist) at a London hospital. She told me that your condition quite definitely needs to be looked into. The sort of thing you describe is unusual in a 14-year-old. Quite simply, it should not be happening. Tests would need to be carried out and you may need some treatment.

This is not meant to frighten you, only to get you moving.

Tell your parents about your problem and get them to contact your family doctor. Your doctor may want to see you first to ask some questions, or he/she may refer you directly to a hospital for tests. If you would rather see a female doctor, make this clear to your parents. Most general practices have at least one female doctor in the team, and in hospitals, male and female staff work side by side. If you are worried about being examined, your mum can stay with you all the time.

Don't continue worrying and suffering in silence. If medical treatment can clear up your condition, you will be much happier in the long run, won't you?

Dear Jo,
I think that I am addicted to chocolates. I can't stop eating them and I am getting fat and my friends tease me. I am really fed up and I don't know what to do. Give me some advice please.

Karen Peters,
Buckingham

I too have a passion for chocolates even though I know they don't do me any good. I find that the best way to resist temptation is to keep them out of the house altogether. Ask Mum and Dad to co-operate. Most adults welcome an opportunity to resist temptation and get healthier too.

Try and find some other treats as a replacement. There is all sorts of splendid fresh fruit around which you can enjoy without being plagued by calories or spots. Fruit salads with nuts are lovely.

Also, award yourself a little prize at the end of a week if you have been really good. One small chocolate bar for example, or a cream cake, but make sure you don't start eating them again on a regular basis.

There is no medical evidence that you can actually become addicted to chocolate, but I have heard that there is a society called Chocoholics Anonymous, so there are obviously plenty of people with your problem.

Dear Jo,
Last month my friend had a cigarette and now she has had about four. I don't know what to do, as she is only 11 and so am I.

She has told her mum, who started when she was seven so she was quite sympathetic, but she can't tell her dad because he would be very upset.

She told me and some of her other friends, but I don't know how to tell her to stop or how stupid she looks, and I don't want to hurt her feelings.

Jane Edwardes,
Bromley, Kent

By now, everyone must be aware that smoking is *very* bad indeed for your health. Tell your friend to look at the warnings printed on the packets if she needs reminding.

Perhaps your friend doesn't realize how nasty she will begin to smell if she continues to smoke regularly. Smokers never do seem to know how they smell to non-smokers — not only their clothes but their breath and hair as well.

I hope your friend's mother as well as being sympathetic, has also told her daughter that she is playing a dangerous game.

Most young people start smoking because they think it looks grown up, but as you say, actually it just looks stupid. Most grown-ups wish they could stop.

If you want to look more grown up, try wearing your hair in different styles and get your mums to buy you some make-up. There are lots of ranges around which are specially designed for young people. Experiment applying it, but don't put too much on or you'll end up looking like children who have raided Mum's make-up bag.

Dear Jo,
We are very worried for a few people in the year above us at school who are 13 and have just started smoking.

They started when they went on a picnic to revise for exams. We are very good friends with these girls. We don't know what to do, because if we tell the teacher, they'll get into trouble.

Libby Jennings,
Sandy Rose,
Durham

Everything I said in my previous reply to Jane, goes for these girls as well. Unfortunately, it is all too easy to become addicted to nicotine and very difficult to get off it. Nicotine is a drug.

Perhaps you could suggest 'smoking' as a topic for the school debating society. This would give an opportunity for different people to ask questions, obtain information and express opinions.

You can't really do more to help your friends. In the end, everyone makes up their own minds what they are going to do.

Dear Jo,
I am a boy of 13 and I am now a smoker. I have tried to stop smoking but I can't. I am dead worried because people have told me all the bad things that can happen to you if you smoke regularly. I want to stop before it's too late. I don't want to tell my mum, because I don't want

her to know I smoke. Please could you give me some advice on how to stop before it's too late.

Darren Daniels,
Leeds

Read the other letters in this section, Darren. The only way to stop is to be very determined that you want to – very determined. No one else can stop for you and I believe that there is no easy way. Try to remember that smoking does you absolutely *no good* at all. It has absolutely nothing to recommend it.

You will certainly be tempted by advertising, by friends who smoke and by cigarettes themselves. Say no to all of them every time. Try sucking sweets or chewing gum for a while as a substitute.

Of course, you have to make sure you keep your teeth clean, but, in the long run, the sweets will do far less damage to your health than the smoking. If you stay off cigarettes, the craving will eventually go.

Work out how much you spend on cigarettes, and then spend your cigarette money on something else; books, tapes, sports equipment. Then you'll be earning yourself a reward for not smoking.

Very, very good luck.

Dear Jo,
I have a very worrying problem. I am 14 years old but I look much older. I go around with a boy of 16 who is very nice and my parents like him. The trouble is that he likes going to pubs. I know that I'm not supposed to drink at

my age and neither is he but I find that I like the effect it gives you. The other night, I had a bit too much (I drink rum and coke) and I was sick in the garden. Luckily, my parents didn't hear me. The trouble is that this hasn't put me off. Does this mean that I am now an alcoholic?

Lesley Cellier,
Milton Keynes, Buckinghamshire

Alcohol, like tobacco, is a drug. The only difference between these two and other drugs like cannabis and amphetamines, is that these two are legal and socially acceptable (although smoking is becoming less so) and the other drugs are not.

You are not an alcoholic (this is a term that isn't used so much now) but it is very easy to travel down a slippery slope.

Alcohol is bad for your body and your mind, especially if you start drinking at such a young age. Unfortunately, young people have a lower tolerance for alcohol than older people (this doesn't mean that it's OK for older people to go and get blind drunk every night). The immature body also builds up tolerance and becomes addicted more quickly on a smaller amount than does the mature body.

You say you like to drink because it feels nice. Perhaps you're a bit shy, Lesley, and it helps to relax you. Try having a warm bath filled with bath oil at home before you go out and perhaps practise some yoga. If you don't want to go to classes you can find out how to do it from books. You'll then feel relaxed before you go out.

You are taking a risk going into pubs and drinking. It is against the law. Is it really worth it?

Why don't you try and persuade your boyfriend to do

something else in the evenings. Go to the cinema and have a take-away afterwards; go round to a friend's house; do a sport. If drink is available, say that you're dieting and have a low calorie Coke or similar. Tell your boyfriend that he's putting on weight and that he ought to cut down on the beers. Perhaps his vanity will help him to keep off the booze.

Good luck.

Dear Jo,

I am 14. My dad and mum often let me have a glass of wine with them when we are having dinner, but they won't let me go into pubs with my friends. I think that if it's OK to drink, then it's OK to drink anywhere. Are they right or am I?

Sam Carter,
Warwick

I think that this is a hard one, Sam. I guess that your parents believe in the French view of alcohol, or in the French view of wine at least. This is that wine is an intrinsic part of family meals. French children have a glass of diluted wine with meals from a very early age — even three and four, when most British children are drinking milk or fruit juice. The argument is that by making wine part of family life and readily available at certain times of the day, the mystique and glamour is removed from it. The trouble is that it is, in a sense, condoning alcohol consumption in children, and is a view open to misinterpretation.

Have you asked your parents their views? I think that would be a good starting point.

Do also remember one simple fact, Sam. Children and young people are often allowed in pubs, but it's not legal for the landlord to sell alcohol to anyone your age. If he did he could be prosecuted.

I'm sure it is the legal point of view which worries your parents, as well as the possibility that you might be tempted to try all sorts of other more powerful drinks than wine.

You're going to be able to drink if you want to, for most of your life. Why put your money in the brewers' pockets now? Spend it on something else.

Dear Jo,
I am 11 years old and I don't know how I am going to get through life if my mother keeps treating me the way she does.

If I just say something polite to her, she starts yelling and shouting at me and sometimes hits me.

When I come home from school at night and say hello to her she sometimes doesn't answer me or she starts yelling at me for forgetting to do something or other. I usually end up crying in my room every night.

I can't speak to my dad about it, because he's usually at the pub and when he comes home he's usually drunk and nasty to me, my brother and sister and my mum.

I have talked to my gran about it, but she can't really do anything.

Helena Knowles,
London

It sounds to me that there are quite serious problems in your family and I would guess that they all relate to Dad's drinking.

This has created a situation that puts everyone on edge. Mum feels rotten and hard done by, so she bites your head off, even though you haven't done anything to deserve it.

I expect everyone in your family is feeling fairly miserable, including Gran.

You have done well to recognize that there is a problem and I hope you will get some help.

I phoned an organization called Al-Anon to find out a bit about them and to see what they could suggest for you. Al-Anon family groups provide support for the family and friends of people with a drink problem.

Al-Anon can help even if the drinker does not admit that he/she has a problem. Quite often, people who drink too much don't think they have a problem. They blame everyone else for things that go wrong.

At Al-Anon group meetings, people can talk about what happens in their families, and try to find ways to help themselves.

Because there are lots of young people whose lives have been affected by someone else's drinking problem, special groups called Alateen have also been formed. These are for teenagers. Again the idea is to try to understand what drinking does to you and your family.

Addiction to and dependence on alcohol, cause very special problems, and you really need people with special understanding to help you.

To find out more about Al-Anon and Alateen, write to the address at the back of this book, or give them a ring to find out where your nearest group is.

Perhaps you could discuss this idea one day with Mum

when she is not feeling too tired, and you could sit down together and ring Al-Anon. They are very helpful and understanding. If you don't feel ready to talk to your mum, then write or phone yourself. I think you'll feel better as soon as you make some contact. Good luck.

I would like to emphasize that Alateen is *not* for teenagers with a drink problem.

If other readers, or their friends, feel that they themselves may have a drink problem and want to do something about it, the people to contact are one of the organizations specifically for people with drink problems, listed at the back of this book.

Dear Jo,

I was staying at my friend's house the other day while her parents were away. Her older sister (she's 17) was supposed to be keeping an eye on us (we're 14). On Saturday evening, she had a couple of friends round and they were smoking something which smelt funny. When I asked my friend what it was, she said, 'Don't worry, it's only dope'. I think she meant marijuana. Isn't marijuana illegal any more? I didn't say anything to my mum and dad or to her parents when they came back. Should I tell anyone? Is it dangerous?

Christina Morrison,
Glasgow

Marijuana (and cannabis) are illegal drugs. I should imagine your friend's parents would be very worried indeed if they knew that their daughter was smoking illegal substances in the family home, for which *they* could be prosecuted, as she is under age. I should think they would also be very upset as they had left their older daughter in a position of trust, looking after you and your friend. It is difficult to know whether you should tell anyone or not. On balance I think that any interference by you would be resented all round.

Cannabis is one of the most controversial of all drugs, not because it is the most harmful, but because many people think it should be made legal. It is not addictive in itself, although it may have harmful effects on the brain and body if used over a long period, but this has not been conclusively proved. On the whole it would appear to be *less* harmful than either alcohol or tobacco.

However (and it's a big however), while cannabis *is* illegal, it could be particularly dangerous to young people, because in order to obtain it they would have to get to know people who sell it and who may themselves be involved in the whole drug subculture.

If your friend asks you to stay the night again, make quite sure that her parents will be at home. If they are not, make some excuse.

Dear Jo,
I am extremely worried, because I think that my oldest brother is smoking crack. I have read in the papers that this is very dangerous. I have told him I knew he was smoking this, and he didn't deny it, he just laughed. I don't want to tell my parents because he'll never forgive me. My

other older brother, Julian, says what could they do anyway. I'm 14 and my oldest brother is 21.

Nicholas Holm,
Northwich, Cheshire

You are right to be worried, Nicholas. Crack is one of the most dangerous of all drugs and particularly appeals to young people. Crack is a purified form of cocaine that is said to give an almost immediate 'high'. Because the intensity of sensation is so short-lived it encourages users to smoke more within a very short space of time. This can lead to a form of addiction within a few days. It is also comparatively cheap, and if you go to the 'right' places, pretty available.

I can understand that you don't want to tell your parents (they may well know anyway), but perhaps you and your middle brother could talk to your older brother together. At least it will show him that you both care about him.

People who take 'hard' drugs tend not to get enough enjoyment out of ordinary, everyday life or are deeply unhappy. I'm afraid that as your brother is an adult, Nicholas, unless he wants to give up, there's probably not a lot you can do to make him.

Why don't you and Julian contact Release or Accept National Services, whose addresses are at the back of this book. They offer help if someone in the family is a drug taker.

Dear Jo,
I go to boarding school. Last week a few of us went down by the river with a picnic. One of my friends suggested that we try some glue-sniffing for a laugh and she'd brought some glue with her. I didn't like it much because it gave me a headache and I felt sick, but my friend said it made her feel great and she still felt great in class much later. She wants to try again, but I don't really. How can I stop her?

Tanya Logan,
Cheltenham, Gloucestershire

Young people have always liked to experiment, but this experiment is one that could do you all a great deal of harm. Perhaps if you tell your friend exactly what glue-sniffing can do to her, it may put her off trying again.

Glue, hairspray, nail polish, correcting fluid, paint stripper, and a few other things all contain substances that when sniffed make you feel wonderful, excited and even give hallucinations. These effects can be short-lived or last a few hours.

The not so nice side-effects can be headaches and nausea (like you experienced), loss of memory, sleepiness and bad temper. But these are nothing compared to the possible long-term effects: liver or kidney failure, anaemia, leukaemia, brain damage and a couple of others. Deaths have actually occurred from heart failure while the substance is being inhaled.

Are these risks worth it for a momentary kick? I hope not. Show this to your friends and talk about it together.

5

LOVE AND ROMANCE

Young people's first ventures into love tend to be incredibly intense and all-consuming. The feelings many of you are experiencing for the opposite sex are new and powerful and often upsetting.

Many of the letters I get from both sexes, are concerned with lack of self-confidence and unrequited love, in about equal portions.

Others are concerned with how to start/end a relationship, the 'right' and 'wrong' ways to behave during a relationship, how to get parents to understand about a relationship and how to cope with having more than one relationship!

Preoccupation with the opposite sex is perfectly normal once you have reached puberty and no one need be worried if they find it difficult to think about anything else.

Early relationships can swing across the entire spectrum from intense happiness to intense misery, but they also provide a very solid base upon which to build the more mature relationships of adult life.

Dear Jo,
I'm very upset because all my friends have got boyfriends and I don't have one. I'm really fat and ugly, and no boys have ever asked me to dance or anything at parties. Once, my friend Cleone and I, organized a disco so that I could meet some boys, but it was no good.

I am 13 years old and I haven't had a boyfriend since I was two!

Vanessa Earlham,
Studland, Dorset

I do very much sympathize with you. You must feel very left out and lonely, but you mustn't despair. You've actually got to make a couple of decisions. Which is more important to you – to have a boyfriend or to eat?

Of course, I understand that you are probably eating a lot and putting on weight because you are miserable, but I'm afraid that it's a vicious circle. You will remain miserable because you are overweight and you don't like being overweight. If you were happy with it you wouldn't have a problem: many very attractive people are overweight and don't feel the need to be anything else. It's all to do with the way you see yourself.

I think that the best thing you can do, is to go into hibernation for a couple of months and change your image.

Ask your mum to help you lose weight by giving you sensible food (I'm sure you know what you should and should not be eating) and by keeping chocolate and sweets and so on out of the house.

Have regular exercise at the same time. If you are very overweight, the pounds will probably drop off.

This will require a huge amount of determination, but if you want to do it, you will.

After a couple of months you will probably look and feel much healthier. You will also be rightly proud of your self-discipline. Get your hair done in a new way; experiment with make-up and you'll be ready to face the world.

You will know that you are looking as good as you can and your self-confidence will show. You're obviously nice as you've got a lot of friends. Start going out with your crowd again and enjoy yourself. If you meet a nice boy, well that's a bonus.

Remember that it's not the boy you go out with who makes you the person you are. You're special all by yourself!

Dear Jo,
I'm 13 and all my friends are paired with really hunky guys. I don't even get looked at and I don't think that I'm particularly ugly.

My friends try to ignore the fact but I feel really out of place at the disco. My friends are all dancing and are having a really great time.

My best friend Sheila has given me some tips, but nothing seems to help. I'm 13 and desperate. What can I do?

Laura Loden,
Blandford, Dorset

Perhaps the problem is that there are no guys that you really fancy at the disco. You say that you feel out of place. Perhaps you'd be better meeting people through some activity rather than at the disco. What are you interested in? See if you can find a class or club to join.

Try to go to parties where you know there might be some new people that you haven't met before. Perhaps some of your friends might enjoy expanding their social groups too.

You just haven't found quite the right social scene for yourself yet.

Dear Jo,

I have a problem with this boy who seems to have taken a fancy to me. Once he tried to get me in the school pool. He keeps on sending me lots of presents but I send them back. I'm afraid that he might have some infection, as he has a lot of boils and bumps etc. Please help me.

Patti Collins,
Uttoxeter, Staffordshire

If you don't like this boy, then you are quite right to send his presents back. The next time he sends you anything, add a little note thanking him for his presents, but telling him not to send you any more, because although you wouldn't mind being friends you don't want any sort of relationship. He should get the message.

I think that it's highly unlikely that he has any sort of infection, the poor boy is probably plagued by acne, which is a skin disorder which happens to some boys when they reach puberty.

It's not his fault, and unfortunately, there's not that much he can do about it in a hurry.

Dear Jo,
I have a problem. At school there's a boy I'm madly in love with. I know you'll probably say, 'Well ask him out then', but it's not as easy as that. He's the kind of boy who wears those neon French wristbands to school even though you're not allowed to, and he goes to all the discos and he goes out with girls in the fourth year. Also, I don't really know him because our classes are not taught together.

My friend and I have made a plan for me to meet him at the next disco. But what if he doesn't ask me out. What can I do?

Bethany Tebbs,
Aberystwyth, Dyfed

It seems to me that you fancy this boy because he is glamorous and a bit of a rebel. He clearly doesn't think much of school rules. Men and boys like this are always very appealing because there is something slightly 'dangerous' about them. You are obviously not the only one who fancies him if he goes out with girls in the fourth year who are presumably older than he is.

Of course, you don't really know what he is like. You may find if you get to know him that you don't really get on with him.

However, go ahead with your plan at the disco. If he asks you out, then you'll soon find out whether you like him or not, and if he doesn't, then I should stop pining for him and turn your attention elsewhere.

Dear Jo,
I love this boy in my school. We used to go to primary school together and we were very friendly. He used to tease me a lot. My friend asked him if he liked me and he said yes as a friend but that he would never go out with me. I have told quite a lot of people that I love him and most of his friends know.

At Christmas I gave him a lovely gold pen, but he sent it back and apparently called me a rude name.

Quite a few boys want to go out with me but I am not at all interested in them. I just want him. We are both 14. What can I do?

Olwyn Evans,
Carmarthen, Dyfed

To be honest, I don't think there's much that you can do. You've made it quite clear to this boy, that you fancy him and would like to go out with him, and you've had your answer. He was clearly prepared to be friendly to start with, but now I am afraid that you may have annoyed him by pestering him. Perhaps he is getting a lot of stick from his friends about you and is embarrassed.

It wasn't very polite of him to call you a rude name when he returned your Christmas present, but maybe he felt driven to it.

You can't force him to fall in love with you and I think that the more you chase him, the faster he is going to run

in the opposite direction. Try cooling things for a bit and
see what happens.

Dear Jo,
My mum doesn't like me using the word 'fancy', but this
has to be an exception.

At school, there is a boy who fancies me. I like him a lot
but I don't fancy him and I never will. I've tried to and I
can't. I'm scared he will ask me out and I don't want to
hurt his feelings by saying no. I already fancy someone
else. What can I say?

Caroline Williams,
Richmond, Surrey

There are times when you do have to be cruel to be kind –
but there is a way of doing things so that the other person
is hurt as little as possible.

If this boy asks you out, you must tell him the truth –
just as you've told me. Just say that you like him very
much as a friend, but that you fancy someone else. If you
make excuses, he'll keep asking you out, and you'll end up
being annoyed with him. Tell him the truth and you may
be able to have him as a friend.

Dear Jo,
I am having a problem with a boy at school. He is always
catching me and following me. My friend says that he

fancies me and I must say it looks like it. I fancy him too. What shall I do?

Melanie Parker,
Hull, Humberside

I don't really see what your problem is; you fancy him and he fancies you – the sort of problem many people would like to have! Perhaps you're worried that he hasn't asked you out yet, in that case, make the first move and ask him. He'll probably be delighted and he won't have to keep following you around any more.

Dear Jo,

I have been going out with David for a year now. When we're together, things are just perfect. The trouble is that he always wants to go to football on a Saturday afternoon, or cricket in the summer. He doesn't mind if I go along, but I'd rather not because I find both games dead boring and he talks to his mates all the time anyway.

I think that he should spend Saturdays with me. We do go out together in the evenings, but I want him around in the daytime as well. What can I do?

Lindsay Burnham,
Port Talbot, West Glamorgan

It's a very good idea that you both continue to enjoy your own interests. It sounds as if you see a lot of each other and it is essential that you both have some space as well.

When David is with his mates, why don't you get

together with your friends? Go shopping, or to an exhibition or go and have a cup of coffee and a chat.

When you and David meet up, you'll have much more to talk about because of your separate activities. And I'm sure that he will appreciate someone who has sufficient independence to respect his freedom as well.

Dear Jo,
I have got a very big problem. At school there are two boys who I like very much but I don't know which one to choose because they both want to go out with me. My best friend has the same problem. We are 12.

Alison Coates,
Worcester

Why don't you go out in a foursome or sixsome until you make up your mind? Perhaps when you get to know them even better you can decide which one you want to go out with.

Alternatively, perhaps you could go out with them both. If you're quite open about it, then I don't see why not. After all, going out a couple of times with someone, doesn't necessarily mean that you are about to get married! After a couple of dates, you'll probably find that you get on better with one than the other, or you may not like either of them!

Dear Jo,

There is a boy I fancy and I think he fancies me. But we don't have the guts to tell each other so he goes out with other girls who ask him; then they show off about him because he is so handsome.

I have attempted to get over this problem by asking my brother to tell him that I like him but my brother just says that he won't interfere with my relationships. What shall I do?

Susie Cuthbertson,
Aberdeen, Grampian

I think that your brother is quite right, Susie. It really is nothing to do with him, and you might blame him if anything went wrong.

Take hold of your courage and ask this boy out. Suggest something casual like going for a hamburger or for a walk down by the river. It sounds to me as if he'll jump at it but you'll never know unless you try.

Think how awful it would be if you never went out with each other because both of you were too frightened to ask.

Dear Jo,

I am 13 and would very much like to have a girlfriend. The trouble is that I am hopeless at chatting girls up. Whenever I am with my friend I just stand there like a dummy and he does all the talking. If I am ever alone with a girl, I am completely tongue-tied. How will I ever get a

girl if I go on behaving like this? I am not too bad looking, just very shy. Please help.

Simon Spencer,
Leicester

Most people are shy even if they don't show it. Some of the noisiest and rowdiest people are really shy. Their noise is just a way of hiding it. Remember too that girls are human beings and are just as shy as boys, as you can probably tell if you read most of the letters in this section.

Try to go around with a group of people, boys and girls, that you know well; then you can practise talking to girls without being under pressure to chat them up. If you genuinely feel interested in what they have to say, then conversation should flow. I shouldn't hang around too much with your talkative friend, otherwise he will always do the chatting and you won't get a chance to try.

I don't think that girls will mind if you're shy, as long as you are sincere. If you could just manage to ask them a few questions and get them talking, you could do most of the listening to begin with, and everybody likes a good listener. Not all girls enjoy a flirtatious line, you know. Sometimes it sounds a bit too practised and puts girls off.

When you meet a girl you really fancy, and you think she fancies you, then I expect you'll find the right words somehow.

Dear Jo,
My boyfriend and I are very much in love. We have been going out for a year now and we want to get married when we are both 16 which is in another year. My mum won't even talk about it. She just says wait and see how you feel in a year. If we want to, can we get married next year? Do you think it's the right thing to do? I'm sure we won't change.

Vivian Paige,
Middlesborough, Cleveland

It is legal in this country to marry at the age of 16, but only with your parents' consent. Without it, you can't get married until you are legally adults, when you are 18.

I think your mum is right. It may seem impossible to believe now, but you may feel very different in a year's time. If you still feel the same, then obviously, there will have to be a lot of discussion with both sets of parents.

If you are asking my personal opinion, then I would say that for most people, 16 is too young to get married. A much greater percentage of teenage marriages fail than in any other age group in the population. That isn't so surprising really. When you are in your teens, you haven't fully developed as a person. You haven't yet discovered all your likes and dislikes nor have you had a chance to see the world. You and your boyfriend may mature in completely different directions. The more you see of life and the more you become familiar with your own character and emotions, the more you'll be sure of the sort of man you want to marry.

If you still feel the same about your boyfriend in a year, then I would suggest that you continue to see each other but also pursue your separate lives. If you are really right for each other then (and it sounds terribly corny) your love will be able to stand up to all the pressures.

Dear Jo,

I am 16 and I have slept around a bit. I've got a bit of a reputation. This hasn't really worried me too much before now, in fact I've rather enjoyed being a 'bad' girl. However, something has happened to make me want to change. A boy has just joined our school and he is wonderful. He's American and really nice and I think that I'm in love with him. I have been out with him a couple of times and I think he's quite keen on me, but I'm worried sick that soon someone's going to tell him something about me and he won't want to go out with me any more. What shall I do? I couldn't bear to lose him.

Jude Phillips,
Brighton, Sussex

It is quite possible that someone *will* tell your boyfriend about your past. Are you ashamed of it? It sounds as if you are. You must therefore tell your boyfriend yourself before anyone else does. You don't have to go into detail. Just tell him that you've made a few mistakes, but that now you've met someone you really like you want to change. If he's really keen on you, he'll appreciate your honesty and it won't make any difference.

I do hope that you've been careful though, Jude? I'm sure that you know all the possible risks of pregnancy, or worse, AIDS.

Dear Jo,
I love my boyfriend very much. We are both 16 and have been going around together for 18 months. The trouble is that now we have reached a bit of a crisis. Mark wants us to sleep together, and is putting the pressure on. I am a virgin, and although I desperately want to sleep with him. I'm frightened about getting pregnant. Mark says that I shouldn't worry because he'll wear a condom, but I know that they're not 100% safe. It's beginning to come between us and I am afraid that if I don't sleep with him he'll give me up and I couldn't bear it. What do I do?

Cassie Clarke,
Luton, Bedfordshire

First of all you have to decide what *you* want to do.

If you don't really, in your heart of hearts, feel ready to sleep with Mark, then you shouldn't. I'm sure it's very difficult if you love each other, but you've got to *both* be ready and sure.

And if you are worried about getting pregnant then you would feel very tense and it wouldn't be a satisfying experience for either of you. I hope that Mark will respect your decision and try not to pressure you further.

If, on the other hand, you feel that you do want to sleep with Mark, then it would be sensible to take adequate precautions. Visit your local Family Planning Organization, or ring one of the numbers at the back of this book. They will advise you on the most suitable form of contraception for you: everything will be in complete confidence. Many of these organizations also have trained counsellors to advise young people.

Dear Jo,
Our names are Jemma and Sally, and we are 15. We are worried because we have both got the same boyfriend and we love him very much. But we're best friends. We have both had dates with Ray (him), and he has given both of us separate reasons for hoping. Who does he love and who will have him?

Perhaps he loves someone else and we are wasting our time.

Can you suggest anything?

Jemma Percival,
Sally Sutcliffe,
London

I should imagine that the one person who is really having a good time at the moment is Ray. What boy wouldn't enjoy two attractive young women fighting over him: and, as you rightly point out, there may be more! Ray is obviously having a good time playing the field at the moment, and if he's the same age as you two, you can't blame him.

Has he got any friends that you might fancy? Or aren't there any other boys in your class or school whom you like?

You both sound too sensible to let suspicion and jealousy spoil your friendship: by all means keep fancying Ray, but remember that at your ages there are plenty of other fish in the sea.

6

SCHOOL LIFE

Until you are 16, 17 or 18, school plays a major part in your life. You spend more time there than anywhere else. You probably have your closest friends at school. How you do at school and how happy you are there will determine the direction of the rest of your life.

However, there comes a time when the demands of school clash with the demands of your personal life. Boyfriend/girlfriend problems, an expanding social life and all the other worries of growing up, in addition to the pressures of exams and school achievement, are often a huge burden for young people. Parents are sometimes unable to understand and help with these pressures and even unwittingly make them worse.

It's worth remembering that there is enough time in the day to have a good social life and work hard as well. It takes a bit of planning and a lot of self-discipline but it can be done. It is important to do the best you can at school; we all know how hard it is to get jobs these days and a few qualifications never did any harm. But it is also important to develop your personality by expanding your social scene and outside interests. Quite a tall order and there may be a few rough patches, but not impossible.

Dear Jo,

I am 14 and in secondary school. I've been having no trouble at school until now when I'm in the fourth year.

Suddenly all my friends have fallen out with me for no reason at all and have started picking on me.

Now they call me names and punch and kick me, and I can't do it back because they go around in groups now and don't like me any more.

I can't go to lessons without the teacher there because they will start to pick on me, not that the teacher does much about it.

Please, please give me some advice – it's urgent.

Paul Chambers,
Bradford, West Yorkshire

If you are being bullied, it is very important that you tell someone – parents, teacher, or the head of your school. Bullying, especially on the scale that you are describing, is very hard to cope with. It needs to be stopped and someone in authority at your school needs to lay down the law in such a way that it won't happen again – to you or anyone else. The bullies must be told to stop, and if they don't, some disciplinary action needs to be devised. So make sure you tell someone every time you are bullied.

Dear Jo,

In school last term, I had good marks for most of my exams. So I had the choice to do German. In the end I decided to do German and drop another subject. But when

I asked all my friends, they weren't doing German, so I know I'm going to be on my own and I won't be able to ask my friends about homework or anything else.

Damian Fielding,
Leith, Lothian

Well, that doesn't sound like a problem. If you are old enough to start German, you are old enough to be working independently. Make sure you work hard in class from day one so you don't miss anything. If you are away from school for a day, you can borrow one of your classmates' books to help you catch up – it would be a good way of expanding your friendship group too. By the end of the year you will be able to feel pleased with your achievement – that you have succeeded on your own.

Dear Jo,
In my school, we do an SMP maths project. It has four levels and I am in the top one. I am almost the best at maths in my class, but my dad doesn't think that I am working hard enough. Other people mess around all lesson, but I work hard and my dad still shouts at me.

I have to do a lot extra in the holidays and after school. It wears me out and I don't have much time to do other homework, so I am in trouble in school as well. I have talked to my head-of-year, but he couldn't help. Can you?

Warren Andrews,
Solihull, West Midlands

I think that you may again have to approach your head-of-year. Explain the problem just as you have in this letter or show it to him and my reply. If he still says he can't help, ask him if he agrees to you talking to your maths teacher and/or your head teacher.

Someone at school needs to realize that you have a problem. Then they can invite your dad to come to school so that you can all discuss it together.

I am sure that your dad wants you to do well at school. Perhaps he thinks that maths is the most important subject for a future career. Whatever the reason for his pressure, he clearly doesn't realize how miserable he is making you feel. Have you talked to your mum? Maybe she could get through to your dad.

Dear Jo,
I have a problem, and so does my friend. We go to an all girls day school and we wonder how we are ever going to meet any boys. We have to do homework every night except Saturday, and then we both have to be in by 10.30 p.m. Lots of the girls in our class are in the same situation. The trouble is that we live miles out in the country and the nearest disco is quite a distance away. Our parents don't mind us going to it, but the last bus home is at 9.30 p.m! What can we do? We are 14.

Patience Owen,
Kendal, Cumbria

Young people in country areas do have problems. I don't think things have improved much over the years. I was brought up in the country so I know what you mean only too well.

I can offer a few suggestions.

Firstly, see if your parents or your friend's parents would object to your having a party. Then invite all your friends from school and get them all to bring one boy. It doesn't matter who they are — brothers, cousins, neighbours or old friends. I am sure that you can all scrape up one each. That way you will all get to meet loads of different boys. *You* may not fancy your brother or cousin, but one of your schoolfriends might.

Second suggestion: try and get your parents and those of your friends to do a rota for collection from the Saturday night disco. I'm sure that they wouldn't object, if it only meant having to pick you up once every three or four weeks. They might even be pleased at the idea, because they would feel confident about your getting home safely. Maybe they would let you stay there an extra half an hour or so if you were all together.

Thirdly, is there a tennis club or other sports club within reach? They tend to be situated out of towns. If so and membership is very expensive, maybe your parents could arrange that one or two of you join, so that the rest could go as guests, and the cost be split between several parents with interested daughters. You're sure to meet someone there, and such clubs usually have a pretty hectic social calendar as well.

Lastly, if all else fails, have you considered going on a residential course in your school holidays? Some of them are very expensive, but not all. Some are run by local councils and cover a huge range of activities from painting to sail-boarding.

I hope you have some success.

Dear Jo,

I am not bad at school and my dad thinks that I will make it to university. He never went and regrets it, so he is especially keen for me to go. The trouble is that what I really want is to go to art school. I am doing my GCSE in art and if I do well I want to go on to A level art, but my father thinks it's a waste of time, and I can't see him letting me go to art college. Also, I think that he thinks my sister let him down. She was supposed to go to university but went to LAMDA (London Academy of Music and Dramatic Art) instead. She wants to be a famous actress. My mum is on our side, but I feel that as my dad has been a bit disappointed once, perhaps I should go to university (if I get in). What do you think?

Chris Burroughs,
Ipswich, Suffolk

I think that the person who should go to university, is your dad. Has he ever considered doing an Open University course? It sounds to me as if he would really enjoy it.

Have you ever spoken to him about wanting to go to art college? Try it and see what he says. If he doesn't think it's a good idea, perhaps your art teacher and your mum could get together and talk to your dad.

Perhaps he thinks that an art diploma isn't worth a great deal in the job world, or maybe he imagines you as a penniless artist in a garret. Maybe when your teacher has a talk with your dad, he or she could list the sorts of jobs that a diploma qualifies you for – graphic design, for example.

I'm sure your dad wants the best for both you and your sister, but I do think that *you* should decide whether or not you want to go to university. If there's no subject you're really interested in except art, then you're not going to do very well there.

7

QUESTIONS OF FAMILY

The difference between families and friends is that you choose your friends but you don't choose your family. Living with a group of people of different ages and different sexes is not easy at any time, however much you may love them. During the highly sensitive adolescent and teenage years, there are bound to be explosions. The famous generation gap really does seem to exist. Parents and children (as I know only too well) sometimes feel that they come from different planets.

Today's families include relationships that, even thirty years ago, would have been uncommon. Stepmothers and fathers and step- and half-brothers and sisters are not at all unusual nowadays. However, the divorces, separations and re-marriages which sometimes result in these new relations and situations are not always easy to deal with or to understand. The new extended family can have many pluses but it can take time to discover them.

Dear Jo,
My mum has just become pregnant, but my dad didn't know until she told him. Why didn't he know already? I'm scared that she might be having an affair with another man. Please can you help me.

Melissa Grant,
Aberdeen, Grampian

There is no reason at all, Melissa, why your father should know that you are going to have a new brother or sister until your mum told him. Women know first because their periods stop and they experience other changes in their bodies which tell them that they're probably pregnant. When they think they are, then they go to the doctor to make sure. The doctor does some tests, and when she is quite positive a woman tells her family that she is pregnant. The very first person she tells is usually the baby's father.

I expect your dad knew that your mum might be pregnant, or maybe it was quite a surprise. Sometimes couples practise contraception (which I have talked about in other parts of this book), and very occasionally it doesn't work. Maybe this happened to your mum and dad. I'm sure you don't need to worry that your mum is having an affair. Tell her what you've told me and I'm sure she'll put your mind at rest.

Dear Jo,
I am the youngest in my family and all my sisters are married. I am 14. I desperately need a bra and I found out about periods from my friend. My mother never told me

about them and when I do get mine it's going to be murder because my mum hates to see her 'babby' growing up. What can I do?

Louise Reilly,
Congleton, Cheshire

Many mothers react like yours, Louise, when their children have left home. It's called 'empty nest' syndrome and your mother is just jumping the gun a bit. I expect she thinks that if she keeps you young, then it will be some time before you too leave the nest. Many mums feel very useless and lost when their children have all left home, especially if they have looked after a very large family for many years (which I guess yours may be as you talk about 'all my sisters').

Try to sympathize with your mum and understand why she's acting like this. At the same time, however, it's obviously important that you should be allowed to grow up normally. I think that perhaps the best thing you could do, would be to enlist the support of one of your older sisters. I expect that they can see exactly what is going on. Maybe they had to go through it a bit too. Get your sister to talk to your mum. She can probably persuade her that you need a bra, and to be properly prepared when your periods do arrive.

If that doesn't work, get your father on your side too. Between all of you, I'm sure your mum will give in and admit to herself that you are growing up.

Dear Jo,

I have a problem. Next year, my brother is coming up to the same school as me. He is really nice, but all my friends call him posh. There is one boy in my class who really worries me and who I think will bully my brother. When my brother comes up, I will be in the fourth year and he will be in the first year. I am in middle school now, so I will only be able to look after my brother for a year before I go to upper school.

All my friends tease me about my brother, because he is clever and polite. They call him a swot, posh, snob and boff. I don't like this because I really like my brother.

Ginny Tooley,
Sudbury, Suffolk

I think that your brother is very lucky to have such a loyal sister. It also means that he must, indeed, be a nice boy.

I'm not so impressed, on the other hand, by the sound of your friends. If they feel that someone is posh because he is polite, or a swot because he is clever, then I think that they need to re-examine their own ideas and values. Why on earth are they so interested in your brother anyway? Haven't they got better things to do with their time? Do they think that you're posh too or do they give you the benefit of the doubt because they like you? They do sound strange friends.

I shouldn't worry too much about your brother coping in his new class. Presumably he is doing OK at his current school? I can't believe your friends are going to go out of their way to torment a boy three or four years younger than they are. I'm afraid that you must let your brother fight his own battles. I'm sure that he'll soon make some friends in his new class who may have a very different idea of his character, provided that your friends don't label him 'posh' and 'swot' in front of everyone.

Tell your friends that they're entitled to their opinion, but that you'd rather they didn't voice it to you, as you find it hurtful. If they're any sort of friends at all, they'll lay off.

Dear Jo,
I am deeply upset. My sister has fallen in love with the bully in my form. They are dating each other. I am 13 and she is 12. I want to separate them, because I don't want her to be upset when he drops her, which he does to all his girlfriends. I have tried to warn her, but she only gets cross and breaks my 'My Little Pony' set. I don't know what to do. I am so upset.

Lucy Field,
London

It seems to me that you have done all you can do. It is always distressing when we see someone we love making what we are sure is a big mistake. The trouble is, Lucy, that, to a certain extent, people have to be allowed to make their own mistakes, because that is the way we learn. I should not interfere any more, but let your sister's relationship run its course. Maybe her boyfriend won't chuck her and she'll make him a better person. If this does happen, then try to get to like him too. Perhaps you could find a boyfriend as well and you could go round in a foursome.

On the other hand, if he does drop her, then she will be upset, but most of us have to go through quite a bit of heartbreak in relationships, as well as happy times. She is very young, so she will get over him. It will be very tempting to say 'I told you so': do try not to. Your affection for your sister should help you do and say the right things.

Dear Jo,
I'm 12 and my parents give me a lot of hassle.

They don't like me going out with boys, and say they won't let me until I'm 15. They make me go to bed at 8.00 p.m. and I'm never even tired. They won't even let me go to the shop down the road on my own.

I'm going to a party soon, that finishes late. My mum wants to 'supervise' the party, and take me home at 9.00 p.m. It only starts at 8.00 p.m! If she sits in at the party it will spoil our fun. The party is not in my friend's house, so her parents won't be there.

Janine Chamberlain,
London

Your parents certainly seem to have very fixed ideas about how they want to bring you up. Some of their rules are for your own protection: others seem to have very little to do with you or your needs.

For instance, some children have gone down to the corner shop and never returned, so that may be a safety rule for you. However, children have got to go out on their own eventually. Too much cotton wool is not a good idea.

How about suggesting to your mum that you go down to the shop in the daytime when she is at home. I'm sure you know that you must never talk to strangers or even allow one to approach you.

8.00 p.m. bedtime does sound rather early for someone of your age. Are you allowed to read until 9.00 or 9.30 p.m? Those are not bad times for someone of your age during the week. Perhaps you could negotiate a later bedtime at the weekend.

Do your parents know any of the parents of your friends? If so, perhaps they could get together to discuss bedtimes and no-go areas so that you all have to abide by the same set of rules.

No dates until 15? How about during the day rather than the evening? Sports events or Saturday afternoon cinema might be all right with them. How about school discos? Everyone goes to them – that's often a solid argument – and school events are usually supervised by school staff.

Now, about this friend's party. It certainly won't be much fun for anyone if your mum comes along to supervise, and to have to leave only an hour after the party starts seems a bit unfair to me. However, I think there should be some adults around, I'm curious to know how or where your friend can arrange a party without her parents. But it's not a good idea. You'd be truly amazed at the things that can happen when a party gets out of hand, particularly if the word goes round the neighbourhood, that a party's being held and you get a load of gate-crashers.

If parents have agreed to a party being held, then they can stay very much in the background, possibly helping with the food and drink, but not actually appearing until absolutely necessary. I do hope the party is fun, but safe for everyone.

Dear Jo,
I get some really crazy punishments at home. If I slam a door, I have to keep it open for two weeks (I am 13 and need some privacy, at least when I am dressing!).

If I am cheeky or rude, I get 100 to 500 lines saying, 'I will learn not to be cheeky or rude to my parents', or something similar. I get these from my dad mostly, and he goes into sulks and doesn't speak for a period of time.

Are these normal punishments for a girl of 13?

Cara Lampley,
Preston, Lancashire

Sounds like your parents set high standards for your behaviour and come down on you hard when you step out of line.

I do think that the punishments sound a little old-fashioned and also a bit pointless, but parents do work out their own rules.

What makes things difficult, is your dad sulking and refusing to talk when he is angry with you. It may help if you and your parents talk about how they expect you to behave, before the next crisis occurs. You should have a chance to have your say. Share your concerns and complaints with each other. Then your parents may be willing to agree new punishments that won't last too long and won't embarrass you.

Docking a bit of pocket money and severely restricting

TV viewing I always find hit pretty hard. If you tell your parents about these suggestions, then they'll *know* you're sincere!

Dear Jo,
I am ten, and my mum and dad are separated and are going to get a divorce. I don't know why. I get very depressed wondering why and I wish that they would tell me. Also, I don't know how to react when my dad picks me up from home.

Marina Dorling,
York

Poor you! Stuck in the middle while two grown-ups fight it out.

Have you told your parents that you want to know why they are splitting up? They might have decided not to tell you because they think that it might upset you. Perhaps they do not realize what a heavy load they are placing on you by not explaining the situation.

Do not think that you are the cause of their divorce, Marina. That is almost never the case. Grown-ups have very complicated relationships and they don't always work out. I bet the one thing you can be quite sure of in this unhappy time, is that both your parents love you very much and would hate you to be hurt.

When your dad picks you up, be quite honest about your feelings. Of course you are glad to see him – he's your father and I'm sure that your mother realizes that your reactions are quite natural.

Show your parents this letter. It may help them to understand your feelings.

Dear Jo,
My parents have just got a divorce and I live with my mum. I'm 14. I see my dad every week, and my dad and mum get on well now that they don't have to live together.

The trouble is that I don't always want to go and see my dad — not because I don't love him, but because he lives quite a long way from home and it means that I can't see my friends or play football for a whole weekend. I don't like to tell him, in case he is hurt. What should I do? My mum says that she can't tell him in case he thinks she is trying to stop me seeing him.

Kevin McNaughton,
Newcastle, Tyne and Wear

It is nice to hear when divorced couples can communicate well with each other. Your mum is right not to interfere in this, Kevin. It's something you must sort out with your dad. I think that quite likely, he may be expecting this kind of thing to happen. You must tell him exactly what you've told me, or show him this letter. It sounds as if you have a pretty good relationship so I think he'll understand.

How about asking him if one of your friends can come with you to stay with him for the weekend. If Dad doesn't have much room, I'm sure you and your friend can sleep in sleeping bags for a couple of nights: it might be good fun. Perhaps your dad would take you both to a football match or the cinema.

I don't suppose he'd mind if you missed the odd weekend. Perhaps you could stay with him for a couple of extra days in the holidays. It sounds as if you, your mum and dad have a pretty good understanding, so I hope that they'll be able to be flexible over arrangements with you.

Dear Jo,
My parents are divorced and don't speak to each other at all. My father used to live abroad so I didn't see too much of him. Recently, he's moved back to England, and now he expects to see my sister and I all the time. The trouble is, we hardly know him. It's like spending weekends with a stranger. He doesn't really know how to talk to us and though he tries hard to be nice, it's a bit put on. Do we have to see him?

Kirsty Donald,
Peterborough, Cambridgeshire

This is very difficult for you all. I think that you must give your father a chance to get to know you both. He's obviously trying hard, but if he's not used to children it may be difficult for him. Why don't you suggest some outings together that would be fun for you all and that you could laugh and talk about afterwards; a trip to the seaside perhaps, a day at a theme park or fun-fair, a trip to a museum or theatre. Perhaps you could go out to a hamburger restaurant for dinner and then maybe play your favourite card games when you get home. If you and your sister secretly plan what you are going to do during your stays with Dad, perhaps things will gradually get easier.

Dear Jo,
My parents are getting a divorce and the trouble is that both my mum and dad want my sister and I to live with them. My dad lives in quite a big flat not far from here. My mum says that we may have to go to court. What will they ask us in court? We would rather live with our mum but we don't want to hurt our dad's feelings because we love him too. I am quite glad that they are getting a divorce because they used to row a lot, but my sister and I do want to still see our dad. What can we do? We know the divorce was nothing to do with us, because both my mum and dad have told us that.

Andrew Patterson,
Strathclyde

How very sad for you all that this is happening. However, Andrew, you may be right to be glad that your parents are getting a divorce, because sometimes two people cannot live together and get on.

It is a great shame that your parents cannot agree who you should live with, to such an extent that they have to fight it out in court. Could they not settle on what is called 'joint custody' with your mum having 'care and control'? This means that both parents would have an equal say in your upbringing, where you go to school, whether you follow any religion and so on, but you would live with your mum and she would make the small decisions in your life, like where to buy your socks, and whether you need a new anorak, for example.

Your dad would have very generous access to you: you might stay with him for one night in the week perhaps, and every other weekend, or perhaps for half the holidays. Don't worry that you won't see your dad, you will. I'm sure that both your parents care for you a very great deal, and your mum won't want to deprive you of a father.

It is good too that your parents are living so close together because it means that there won't be any problems going to school or seeing friends.

Of course, I don't know the circumstances of your parents' divorce, but unless there are very unusual reasons, judges tend to leave children in their mother's care. As a general rule, I think it is better if children do not have to appear in court, but judges and lawyers are very understanding nowadays and you would not have to appear in a great big court room but probably in the judge's chambers (room) with only a couple of people present.

If you want to know more about your situation, why not ring the Children's Legal Centre, whose number is at the back of this book. They look at all problems from the children's point of view and are very kind and helpful. They have a lot of leaflets, too, which they could send you.

I do hope everything works out well for you.

Dear Jo,
In my group of friends, I am the only one whose parents are divorced. I don't particularly mind this because they divorced when I was very young and they are good friends

now. My dad has married again and I now have a half-brother and sister who I love a lot. I live with my mum.

The trouble is that some of my friends tease me because we are not very well off. My mum says that my dad gives us all he can, but he's got his other family as well. My mum works too but only part-time, so that she can be with me. I am an only child. How can I stop this teasing; it's getting on my nerves.

Ben Weston,
Rugby, Warwickshire

Well, Ben, I think that the people who have the problem here are not you and your family, but those friends who tease you.

Your dad and mum have clearly managed things well, have a great deal of respect for each other and do the best for you that they can. You obviously have a lovely brother and sister and a lot of friends. I think that you are quite happy with your situation except for your friends' teasing.

Quite frankly, they don't sound like very good friends to me. If I were you, I shouldn't bother to see them any more if their values are so peculiar. It may sound corny, but they should realize that loving family relationships are a great deal more important than two holidays a year and a swish car. I do hope that their family relationships are as good as yours!

If you do want to continue to be friends with them, I suggest that you tell them exactly what you think of their set of values, and tell them to stop teasing you immediately. If they don't, then drop them, and stick with the friends who are a little more sensitive.

Dear Jo,
I am deeply distressed. I am aged 16, quite good-looking and I have had several boyfriends. The trouble is, that when I get friendly with them, they go away.

I am the result of a rape, and I've never seen my father, not that I want to after the way he treated Mum. I don't like to trouble Mum about sex, because of her experience.

Please, please help me.

Sharon Rolands,
Bristol, Avon

You obviously love your mum very much, and are very protective of her because of her bad experience. But I do think that you should 'trouble' her with your problems. I don't suppose she would like you to think that all men and boys are like your father. They're not, as I expect you realize.

Possibly, your relationships haven't worked out yet because you are still quite young. Teenage girls have a lot of friends and boyfriends. Don't be in too much of a hurry to find the 'right' person.

Perhaps you come over as rather 'heavy' to some of your boyfriends and they're not ready for that sort of commitment yet.

Try going around with a gang of friends, both boys and girls so that you get to know boys as friends.

If you would like to speak to someone else about your situation, contact your local Child and Family Guidance Centre via your local council or ring the National Association of Young People's Counselling and Advisory Services, whose number is at the back of this book.

8

PIC 'N MIX

Many of your problems are very serious and possibly more widespread than the number of letters I receive about them indicates. There may be many young people who find it difficult to put pen to paper to express a very personal problem. I hope that some of these letters and answers may help them.

Dear Jo,
I have a horrible feeling that I might have breast cancer.

I sometimes get a nagging sort of pain in the right side of my breast. It hurts when I breathe in deeply or when I run.

I don't want to tell my mum because I'm sure she would want to take me to the doctor. What can I do? I'm 13.

Carrie Davidson,
Leeds

Let me say, first, that if you do find a lump or anything unusual in one of your breasts, it is *not* likely to be anything as serious as cancer, but it should always be checked out.

I contacted a breast specialist at a London teaching hospital. He assured me that breast cancer at 13 is 'virtually unknown'. The earliest case he had come across was that of a 19-year-old, but even that was very early. Breast cancer is more typically found in women over the age of 30.

The specialist also told me that pain is *not* usually a sign of early breast cancer. Your pains are probably caused by normal growth and development of the breasts (the hormones that cause periods to start also cause tender breasts).

So how about visiting your family doctor? Most of what happens to our bodies is quite normal, and these pains soon pass. But it is important to discuss any changes with someone who can give us an informed answer.

If your family doctor is a man and you would rather be examined by a woman, then ask if you can be. As I said earlier in the book, most practices have at least one woman doctor on the team.

Breasts do feel lumpy and that's normal. Get used to the shape and feel of your own breasts, and you will be able to notice if there is anything unusual.

You probably have nothing to worry about, but do go and visit your doctor, just to be sure.

Dear Jo,
I am 14, and my mum still tries to dictate what I wear out of school. Unfortunately, her tastes and mine are not the same. What can I do?

Amanda Beech,
Ruislip, Middlesex

Presumably, your mum pays for your clothes, so it does give her rather an advantage. However, I think that you and your mum must sit down and have a good chat. Perhaps you could reach a compromise. Maybe if your parents gave you a small allowance each month, you could buy what you liked with that. Any big items, like coats and shoes, you could shop for with your mum. You could choose what you liked and she could have power of veto. I am sure that if you take her to your favourite shops, you will soon find things that appeal to both of you.

Dear Jo,
I desperately want to be a vet, but the awful trouble is that I am not very good at science subjects at school. Is there any hope for me?

Charlotte Greene,
Ashford, Kent

I have to be honest, Charlotte, I looked into this and apparently, there is such demand for places at the few veterinary colleges in this country, that they can afford to pick the students with the very best science grades. And I am afraid that science subjects would be required at A level. Any combination of subjects from biology, physics, maths, applied maths or chemistry would be acceptable and A's and B's would be needed. Apparently, it is harder to become a vet than a doctor.

If you want to work with animals, I'm sure that there are other things you can do. Animal nurses work with vets, and they are accepted for training with lower academic qualifications. Or you could try working for an animal charity, such as the RSPCA or the Blue Cross. This is very rewarding and you would know that you were working for very good causes. Have a word with your career teacher at school and see what he/she suggests.

Dear Jo,
I watch *Neighbours* every day and I can't stop thinking about Mike. I am really involved with the programme and worry about what's going to happen each day. I find it difficult to think about anything else. I know that these are

not real people but I can't seem to help it. Am I going mad? I'm 12.

Eva Petrocelli,
London

The producers of the programme would be delighted to hear about you. And of course you're not alone, there are millions like you.

Soaps are designed to hook people, and *Neighbours* is more successful than most.

I once heard watching television described as 'a conscious decision to waste time', and that's exactly what it is. While you're sitting in night after night getting involved with Mike, you could be out enjoying friends and getting ready to be involved with someone real. When that does happen you'll find you're not remotely interested in the programme any more, because what's happening in your own life is so much more exciting than anything on television.

You're certainly not mad: you just have a very bad case of soap addiction and you need to become unhooked quickly. Just turn that set off at 5.30 p.m. You'll soon find it's very painless.

Dear Jo,
I have just started my periods and I am now very frightened that if I get attacked on the way home from school or when I am out with friends, and I am raped, I will have a baby. I am 11.

Susanna Leigh,
Stroud, Gloucestershire

Most women and girls fear being raped. This is not a silly fear because it happens so often today, as we read in the newspapers. It is very necessary to take as many precautions as possible when you are by yourself. I am sure that your mum has told you what they are: never talk to strangers: never walk down unlit streets in the dark on your own: always travel in pairs or more on the train, and so on.

Perhaps you could also go to self-defence classes. Many councils run a variety of different courses and I am sure that you could find one that you would both enjoy and benefit from. More and more girls go to these courses, and I am sure that you would feel much more confident about being out and about if you knew that you could deal with any potential attack. If you were unfortunate enough to be raped and become pregnant, you would be allowed to terminate the pregnancy.

Dear Jo,
My friend and I are lesbians. When we see and leave each other we kiss, and when we go to sleep at each other's houses, we try and have sex. Both of us are too scared to tell our parents. Please help us.

Tanya Mulroney,
Sarah Vawdon,
Birmingham

You don't say how old you are, but in early adolescence you are just beginning to discover your own sexuality and it is quite usual to want to explore sexual feelings with a member of your own sex. This does not necessarily mean you are lesbian — nor does it mean that you are not. It's probably too early to tell.

It may be that as you get older, your sexual feelings will change and become focused upon males, or you may remain as you are.

I'm sure that your parents won't stop loving you whatever you are.

Dear Jo,
I've just started going out with boys and I'm very worried about catching AIDS. I know you can get it during sex, but can you get it through snogging?

Jane Milner,
Exeter, Devon

You are quite right to be worried about AIDS, but it is necessary to get things into proportion. It's not like colds or flu which you can catch by just being in the same room as the sufferer.

Certain body fluids can contain the AIDS virus. Semen and vaginal secretions are the two that everyone knows about. The virus has to enter the bloodstream in order to infect someone. Thus a person can be infected during intercourse either through the tiny cuts and tears which occur inside the vagina, or the virus can be absorbed.

Traces of the virus have been found in saliva. So, strictly speaking, it is possible that French kissing could transmit the disease. This is probably pretty unlikely, but it would be just possible if infected saliva got into the bloodstream through cuts or sores on the tongue, lips, gums or throat.

If you want more information on AIDS, Jane, then ring the Terrence Higgins Trust whose number is at the back of this book. They can tell you everything you want to know.

9

USEFUL ADDRESSES

PHYSICAL AND SEXUAL CHANGES

Health Education Authority
78 New Oxford Street
London
WC1 1AH
Tel: 071-637 1881

They have many pamphlets and books on health related problems.

Family Planning Association
27–35 Mortimer Street
London
W1N 7RJ
Tel: 071-636 7866

They have books and leaflets on aspects of sex and sexuality. They will also have the address of your nearest birth control or youth advisory clinic.

Brook Advisory Centres
153A East Street
London
SE17 2SD
Tel: 071-708 1234

These are birth control clinics especially for young people. They can also give help and advice with pregnancy and relationship problems.

EMOTIONAL UPHEAVALS

National Association of Young People's
Counselling and Advisory Services
(NAYPCAS),
17–23 Albion Street
Leicester
LE1 6GD
Tel: 0533-554775

They can give the address of a young persons' organization near you who may be able to offer help.

Relate
Herbert Gray College
Little Church Street
Rugby
CV21 3AP
Tel: 0788-73241

They can offer help on any kind of relationship or sexual problem.

Children's Legal Centre
20 Compton Terrace
London
N1 2UN
Tel: 071-359 6251

They provide free legal advice to young people from the young person's point of view.

Samaritans

There are many branches throughout the UK. They can help with any problem. The numbers are in the local phone book.

PREGNANCY

British Pregnancy Advisory Service
Austy Manor
Wootton Wawen
Solihull
W. Midlands
B95 6BX
Tel: 05642-3225

They are a non-profit-making charity. They offer totally free and confidential pregnancy tests, sex counselling, birth control advice and supplies, pregnancy and abortion advice. Look it up in your local phone book or contact the above address for your nearest branch.

Pregnancy Advisory Service
11–13 Charlotte Street
London
W1P 1HD
Tel: 071-637 8962

They offer much the same service as the above but are London based.

GAY

Parents' Enquiry
16 Honley Road
London
SE6 2HZ
Tel: 081-698 1815

They offer help to young people or their parents about coming to terms with someone in the family who is gay.

London Gay Switchboard
Tel: 071-837 7324

For someone who is gay or thinks they might be gay and needs someone to talk to.

AIDS

Terrence Higgins Trust
BM AIDS
London
WC1N 3XX
Tel: 071-831 0330

They provide counselling and information on all aspects
of AIDS.

FAMILY PROBLEMS

National Stepfamily Association
162 Tenison Road
Cambridge
CB1 2DP
Tel: 0223-460312

They provide advice and support for step-parents and their
children.

National Council for the Divorced and Separated
13 High Street
Little Shelford
Cambs
CB2 5ES
Tel: 020639-6206.

They will offer help to anyone involved in a divorce or
separation.

Al-Anon Family Groups
61 Great Dover Street
London
SE1 4YF
Tel: 071-403 0888

They provide help to understand and cope with the problems of having an alcoholic in the family.

Alcoholics Anonymous
PO Box 1
Stonebow House
York
YO1 2NJ
Tel: 0904-644026

These are local self-support groups for the drinker who wants to give it up.

Accept National Services
200 Seagrave Road
London
SW6 1RQ
Tel: 071-381 3155

They give advice and addresses on any drink or drug problem.

Release
1 Elgin Avenue
London
W9 3PR
Tel: 071-289 1123
      071-603 8654 (emergency)

They can help with drug, legal and abortion problems.

Also in Plus

DOUBLE TAKE
June Oldham

When unemployed actress Olivia Quinn takes part in a small
television news item about a missing girl, she triggers a series
of dramatic events. Not only is she subjected to harassment,
violence and prejudice, but events start to take on a disturbing
similarity to those surrounding the missing girl's disappear-
ance.

A SEAL UPON MY HEART
Pam Conrad

At the age of sixteen, Darcie suddenly becomes acutely aware
of the lack of knowledge she has of her father. While her
mother is away with her new husband, Darcie spends the summer playing detective to his whereabouts. She also finds friendship in the form of Roman, the seal-keeper at the zoo where
she has a summer job. He charms her as if she is one of the
animals, but is her infatuation with him perhaps going a little
too far?

BIANCA
Joan Phipson

The first time they see her, Emily and Hubert catch no more
than a glimpse of the girl's terrified face as she and her rowing
boat loom briefly out of the mist, before it disappears back
across the water. But it's a face which haunts them both and
they quickly become deeply involved with this strange girl and
her mysterious past.

SATURDAY NIGHT
Hunter Davies

What I'm trying to do, is to get off with this girl called Isabella. There, I mentioned her name. I'll have to lie down now. I know, I'll play with my word processor. A bit of harmless fun, like telling you about those wild parties I've just been to, and these girls who just can't control themselves in my presence. It'll kill a bit of time, till my Isabella comes along. Perhaps this Saturday night . . .?

THE EMPTY SLEEVE
Leon Garfield

At the age of fourteen, Peter Gannet is apprenticed to a locksmith in Covent Garden but his desperate longing to escape from the insufferable adults around him and go to sea lands him into some dubious undertakings. Before long, the old ship's carpenter's prophecy comes true, when in the locksmith's workroom he meets a phantom with an empty sleeve. A gripping thriller about ghosts, a wall of hands, envy, dishonesty and finally murder!

FOLLOW A SHADOW
Robert Swindells

Tim South is fifteen and finding real life particularly uncomfortable – nothing about it measures up to the colourful fantasy world of his imagination, and hanging out with the tough guys is only making things much worse. However, when he stumbles across a faded picture in the attic of a mysterious young man who looks remarkably like him, Tim becomes obsessed with discovering his identity, sparking off a chilling chain of events that will change his life for ever.